Jack and the Ultimate Dare

Anita French

Onwards and Upwards Publishers

4 The Old Smithy London Road, Rockbeare,
EX5 2EA, United Kingdom.
www.onwardsandupwards.org

First edition, published in the United Kingdom by Onwards and Upwards Publishers Ltd. (2022).

ISBN:	978-1-78815-878-7
Typeface:	Sabon LT
Artist:	Josh Williams

Dedicated to Isobelle and Max –

may you always have a love for reading

Jack and the Ultimate Dare

Contents

Jack and the Ultimate Dare

1

Jack and 'The Reds'

"Mummy! Jack has pulled the head off my doll again!"

Jack smiled to himself. *That little sister of mine is so easy to tease,* he thought.

Ella was running down the stairs with tears in her eyes, showing her mum the broken toy.

"Not again... Tell Jack he has to fix it," Mum said with a sigh.

Jack had heard his mum but had no intention of fixing the doll. Why should he? Ella shouldn't be so careless to leave her toys lying around where they could be taken. But he knew he would have to smile and say as much to his mother. It was time to get ready for school, and Jack had to help get everyone ready, much to his disgust. With Jack being the oldest at fourteen, he had to help get his sisters and baby brother dressed and make breakfast for them. It was hard for his mum to do all the work as she was on her own now. His dad had died the previous year in a car crash, and this had made it difficult for the family in lots of ways. Jack had to step up and be the man of the house and never had time to think about what had happened to his dad.

"I'm coming, Mum!" Jack ran down the stairs and grabbed his bag and lunch box.

His mum and siblings went to the car, and Jack waved to them on his way walking to school. They lived in a crowded council estate near the city centre. It wasn't a rough area like some council estates in the north of England where you had to watch your back whenever you left your house in case you would be mugged or something. Here in the outskirts of Swindon, it wasn't dangerous as such but it sure wasn't posh. Jack had lived there all his life so he didn't know any different, but he did sometimes wish they could have some more stuff. His friends weren't wealthy but they did seem to have computer games and cool clothes. Jack didn't have any of that. He had got used to buying clothes in second-hand shops and not having a gaming console, although he secretly wished he could be rich one day and never have to worry about money. He saw how his mum was continually counting the pennies and barely making it through each month. Jack knew that this was not a life for him. He was going to get money – one way or another.

In school Jack was seen as the leader of his friendship group, and some people started to call them 'The Reds' as they all wore expensive red trainers. It was like their sign of belonging, and for some it would take months to save up to buy them, but it would be worth it to be part of Jack's gang. They liked the nickname 'The Reds' and so let it stick. At first, they were getting into trouble with the head teacher for wearing non-uniform shoes, but they had been sent to detention so many times without changing shoes that the head finally gave up and let it slide. Being in Year 10, they were well established in school, and any newcomers soon knew who they were and that it was best to stay out of their way. Jack loved walking down the hall and seeing the youngest in school hide behind bins or tables to avoid being seen by him. He was quite tall for his age with broad shoulders and muscly legs. His red-brown hair was easy to spot, and there were plenty of girls secretly in love with him, as he was truly handsome with his bright, steely blue eyes. At breaktime he would play rugby and was also part of the school's wrestling team, which gave him strength and agility. The power he got from people being frightened of him was exhilarating, and he would scare them on purpose to make them jump and then laugh out loud.

He didn't mind the lessons so much, but he found English particularly tedious. His teacher was always talking about 'grammar this' and 'fronted adverbial that'. It was just confusing and an incredible snooze-fest. Jack would often take to sitting in the back of the classroom and put his book up in front of him – the book standing up, opened – then lay his head in his arms to have a sleep, hopefully undetected. But his plan wasn't always successful.

"Jack Hart, can you please tell me how to construct a sentence correctly according to the model we have just learnt? Jack?" Mr Ross walked up to Jack's desk. "I see that Mr Hart is somewhat tired today," he smiled. "Come on, Jack; if you stay asleep all lesson, you won't have a chance of passing the exam at the end of the year. I really don't want to see you fail, or anyone else for that matter." Mr Ross looked around the room to get everyone's attention. "I know this can be boring, but I promise it will make sense if you just try it. If we all work really hard on this grammar stuff, then I promise we can watch some funny videos online after. What do you say, guys?"

Jack loved walking down the hall and seeing the youngest in school hide to avoid being seen by him.

Jack rolled his eyes and put his head in his arms. *Here he goes again with his inspirational speeches and trying to bribe us to do more work. That might work on the other more gullible students, but not me. Please just get me out of here,* he sighed to himself.

At break time The Reds used most of their time going to find other kids who were scared of them and made them give them money or pulled pranks on them. The favourite gag they did on the Year 7's was to spray water on their trousers in the bathroom and then call out in the hallway, "Look, Harold has wet himself! Hahaha…" The boys would be falling about laughing, and Jack was the one who laughed the hardest and loudest. The poor Year 7 boy would be mortified and run down the hall trying to hide, and Jack and his friends would shout after him.

When they were in the mood for pranks, Jack was usually the instigator and would carefully choose which child they would pick on, and the more insecure and afraid they looked, the more fun it was to tease them. Although deep down Jack knew that their victims might not enjoy it as much as they did, he couldn't help laughing every time they bullied a child, and he suppressed any feelings of empathy or remorse. In fact, the more they cried or looked scared, the funnier he thought it was. He was often told off by teachers on the few occasions he got caught, but it didn't matter what they said. They would put him in isolation for an hour, and Jack usually used that time to have a nap. He wasn't sorry for what he had done, and he would most likely do it again the next day.

Schoolwork was simply boring for Jack, and as he liked challenges, he would find it in other ways. He made it his mission to get back at the teachers who he felt were just there to get at him. They were always saying he could do better and that he needed to work harder if he wanted to be successful in life. It only made Jack *not* want to work more, as he hated having someone tell him what to do. As retaliation, he would steal a few things from school. It started with just a ruler that he snuck in his bag or a mug from the cafeteria. Then he became braver and attempted to take bigger things. Once he even stole a chair! He got one of his friends to distract the teacher by acting up in class, so that the teacher would have to take him into the hall and, when out of sight, Jack could toss the chair out of the window and collect it after the lesson. Whenever he got away with it, it was such a rush that he almost felt addicted to doing it again. Everyone in school knew that it was him who had done it though, and possibly some teachers knew too. But they had no evidence so they couldn't prove it.

As Jack and his friends were sat in the dining hall one day eating their packed lunch, someone walked in the room who made everyone go quiet and stare. Jack's friend Niall nudged him and said, "Look who it is! It's Kane from The Daggers." Jack swallowed hard as he saw the menacing seventeen-year-old walking towards him. Kane used to go to their high school but had been suspended enough times that he had now dropped out. His gang, 'The Daggers', were notorious in their neighbourhood, as they would intimidate anyone who approached them and they were known to be involved in some criminal activities like burglaries and shoplifting. Jack wondered why they were here and was scanning the room for any teachers, as Kane would most certainly be kicked out if he were caught.

Kane walked up to their table and pulled a chair out, scraping the floor as he did, making a screeching sound.

He turned it around backwards and sat on it staring at Jack intently. There were also two friends with him that stood at either side of him with their arms crossed, looking angry and like his bodyguards.

"Now then, Jack Hart. I've heard some things about you. You like nicking stuff?" Kane gave a broad smile, but his eyes were still threatening.

Jack sat up straight and decided not to be scared of this guy. "Yeah, I have had my fair share of taking a thing or two. What's it to you?"

The leader of The Daggers leaned forward on the table and said in almost a whisper, "I'm looking for some new recruits. How do you feel about accepting a dare? *The Ultimate Dare,* in fact." He paused to see what the reaction would be.

Jack nodded and replied, "I'm listening."

Pleased that he had got the answer he was hoping for, Kane went on. "I dare you to steal something really valuable. Something that would show that you would be worthy of joining me. I need someone who has guts and is willing to do what it takes to get the job done. I'll be back in one week, and you can present to me what you've got. Impress me and you can get a share of our next take. There's a lot of money on offer if that's something you are into." It was a rhetorical question, as Kane knew that he was all about getting cash – and the easy way. Most small time thieves were.

Jack thought for a moment. This could be dangerous, and he had never done anything like this before. But he did want to get rich someday, and it wasn't looking like there would be a way of doing that any time soon – and it would be hard work. Plus, he was excellent at stealing stuff and he loved the thrill of it. Maybe it was time to try something more advanced.

Jack stood up and proclaimed, "I'll accept your dare. See you in a week."

Kane gave a wink and a smile and stood up from his chair. His goons hadn't said a word the whole time, and now the three of them walked off. Jack's friends, who had sat in awe and silence for the duration, were now chatting excitedly at the prospects of their mate joining The Daggers. They were impressed and Jack nodded agreeingly – although there was a part of him deep down that made him feel unsettled.

After school he walked home with his friends, and on their way they saw some guys from another class. One of them was Ralph, who was a bit of a hothead. If he got angry, everyone would know about it as he would throw chairs and tables around the classroom and shout rude words. Ralph was known to have no mercy, and there were even rumours that he had killed his cat. They weren't sure if it was entirely true, but looking at him, they would believe it. Most of the time they would leave each other alone, but occasionally Ralph would be in the mood for a fight and mess around with The Reds.

Jack was going to try to avoid them and crossed over the road, but it was too late. Ralph, along with his friends, caught up with them and stood right in front of Jack, puffing up his chest and staring at him with evil eyes. Jack tried to make himself tall as well, although he was shorter than Ralph, and looked him straight in the eye.

Ralph said scoffingly, "Hey, Jack, what you doing around here? Waiting for your mommy?" He burst out in an evil laugh and pretended to suck his thumb, taunting Jack, and his buddies joined in.

Jack just glared at him angrily and pushed him out of the way.

As Jack watched them walk off, he looked across the street and saw an elderly man mowing his lawn. Jack recognised him and then he spotted something. Something valuable. A brand new bicycle. That would be worth at least £1,000.

'Old Man Sam' is what the boys called him, and they had vowed to have him as their enemy forever. Sam had once seen the boys stealing sweets from the corner shop and called the police. They found out who had snitched on them and since then they had made efforts to prank Old Man Sam whenever they could. They had keyed his car, and at Halloween they threw eggs at his house. Once they even posted some dog poo through his letterbox. They signed a note with it saying "Reds", so he probably knew it was them, but they didn't care. He was just a frail old man who was a pain to their existence. Not only that but he was always talking about how he believed in God and that "Jesus loves us". It was so ridiculous, it made Jack's blood boil with anger. *God is about as real as flying unicorns.* Sam was just an old, confused man who deserved anything he got.

Jack turned to his friends. "That's it! That's the valuable item I will steal to get my place in The Daggers." He pointed to the bike that was parked in the garage with the door wide open. Taking it now would be risky as it was in broad daylight, but at the same time this was such an opportunity as the door was left unrestricted and this was a particularly quiet street. Hardly anyone was about, and most people who lived here were either old or at work. It had to be done now!

Once they had a plan ready, they spread out to their positions. Jacob and Niall were chosen to be the distraction and set off to speak to Old Man Sam. The garage was to the side of the detached house, which had no other houses next to it, just trees and bushes. It was a leafy and undisturbed street, and you could tell that Old Man Sam liked looking after his garden. He was quite old, probably in his seventies, and was milling around pruning his rose bush in between mowing his front lawn. There was no gate obstructing the garage, and with the door completely unlocked, it was like he was asking for the bike to be stolen.

Jack and two other boys were hiding behind a tree and watched the others go and speak to the old man. When they seemed to have gained his attention and made him turn his back to the garage, Jack signalled to his friends to go from tree to tree on the street until they snuck up to Old Man Sam's garage. They felt like ninja burglars and were just about to grab the bike and run when one of the boys whispered, "The wheel is locked!" Then they heard Old Man Sam saying, "Let me just show you something in the garage..."

Jack and his friends froze. They were going to get busted.

2

The Freedom Ride

"Oh, wait! Please tell us more about your life as a child, sir." Jacob quickly tried to get Old Man Sam to not go into the garage. It seemed to work, as Sam stopped in his tracks and started telling a story about old times.

Jack and the boys in the garage breathed a sigh of relief but still weren't sure what to do with the lock, and they looked around for something that might be used to cut it open. The lock wasn't even a lock, just a cable-tie tied around each wheel, stopping them from turning so it would be impossible to wheel the bike out of the garage easily. However, it wasn't attached to anything, so that was good, at least. They could hear that Jacob and Niall were running out of things to talk to Sam about and knew that soon Old Man Sam would suspect that something was wrong.

Jack had to act fast so he said, "Let's just carry it out and work out how to cut off the cable-tie later!"

The three boys lifted the bike as quietly as they could and tiptoed out of the garage. They then ran as fast and quietly as they could, although a bit awkwardly as the bike was quite heavy and it was tricky having three people carrying it. They managed to go around the corner unnoticed and then quickly pegged it down the street. No-one was about, luckily, so there were no witnesses.

Jacob and Niall saw the boys were getting away, and once they were out of view, they quickly ended their conversation with Old Man Sam and ran after them. Once they were a few streets away, the gang found a woodland area which they ran into to hide their loot. Now that they felt safe and that they had got away with it, they started laughing and high-fiving each other.

"That was so close, man!" Niall said. "At one point I'm sure that Old Man Sam thought something was up, but we managed to keep on talking about football and his garden, and he just kept jabbering on."

Jack was on a high from managing to get away with his steal; this was the most significant thing he had ever stolen before, and surely he would now win the dare! Previously they had taken a few chocolate bars from the corner shop but never something as valuable as a bike. "That'll teach that Old Man Sam not to mess with us! Hahaha, we have truly put him in his place. Reds rule!" Jack laughed. "I can't wait to show Kane; this will be an impressive steal for sure!" The boys cheered and laughed and jumped around.

Once things had quietened down a bit, Jacob said, "So where are we going to keep the bicycle?"

Jack had always wanted a bicycle and had never had one as his parents could not afford one. He looked at the two-wheeler they had just taken; it looked so new with its shining black metal and golden accessories. Something in him wanted to keep it for himself so badly, and he knew he had to convince his friends that he would look after it.

"That's no problem," Jack said, shrugging his shoulders. "We can keep it in my shed in my back garden. My mum never goes in there so she wouldn't find it."

The other boys seemed to agree that this was the right solution and they decided to meet later on when it was dark to move it from the woods to Jack's house. They didn't want to be seen with it in broad daylight. It was too risky, especially if PC Thomas would see them, as they had been in trouble with him for shoplifting before. After deciding a time, they all split off into different directions and went home. Jack walked towards his house, still feeling the adrenaline from the bust but also having a heavy niggly feeling deep down. He decided to ignore it and kept on walking.

It was just after dark, and Jack told his mum that he was going out for a bit to see his friends.

Jack's mum looked at him and asked, "Where are you going? It's a bit late, isn't it?"

Jack avoided eye contact with his mother. "We are practising for a play at school and we have to learn our lines by tomorrow. I won't be long, I promise," he lied.

"OK then, but be back no later than eight o'clock," said his mum.

"I will!"

Jack ran out of the door. He kept on running fast for the next ten minutes. Jack didn't like lying to his mum, but there was no way of telling her the truth. Running helped him focus on something else, and after a while he was out of puff and stood for a minute catching his breath. As his breathing was starting to become regular again, someone was coming towards him. At first he thought it was one of his friends but then he froze. It was PC Thomas!

The police officer was walking straight towards him, and Jack started to get sweaty hands; his heart was beating even faster than it had after his sprint. Thomas was the local policeman who seemed to know everyone in town. He didn't tend to arrest anyone as such and always seemed to patrol on his own, which was unusual. Jack remembered all too well when PC Thomas had found him and his friends shoplifting at the corner shop near school. The PC had been waiting outside of the shop and caught them when they walked out. He had threatened to take the boys to the station but then seemed to change his mind and said that if they returned the stolen goods, he would let them off with a warning. He was tall, skinny and middle-aged, with a bushy moustache that suited the stereotype of a man in blue. He was always on guard, ready to be of assistance to anyone who needed help, be it old ladies crossing the road or chasing down pickpockets who had stolen someone's wallet. The law was everything to him, and he would make sure that anyone around him would follow it; anything for the safety of the community.

There was nowhere to hide as the policeman approached Jack, and Jack was walking directly towards him.

"Is that you, Jack Hart?" Thomas asked kindly and stood close up to him as if to look him straight in the eye.

Luckily for Jack, it was quite dark out, so PC Thomas couldn't see his nervous eyes or the sweat dripping from his forehead. He cleared his throat. "Yes, sir," he said quietly.

There was nowhere to hide as the policeman approached Jack.

"Hmm... What are you doing out here after dark? You really need to be careful as you never know who can be about, especially in those woodland areas up there." The policeman looked at Jack and seemed genuinely concerned, which made the ordinarily confident Jack feel on edge.

"I'm just meeting some friends, not going anywhere dodgy, I promise." Jack clenched his hands and hoped that the policeman would leave soon.

"That's good. Well, you wouldn't happen to know anything about Sam Green's bike, would you? He reported it stolen this afternoon. It seems that someone stole it straight out of his garage. Burglars these days have some nerve, I tell you. Just wondering if you had heard any rumours or anything?" The PC watched Jack as he waited for him to reply.

Jack was holding his breath and tried to stay calm; he eventually managed just to say, "Nope, don't know anything." He did his best to keep his cool and started to keep on walking. "Good night, sir," he said and walked on towards the meeting point where his friends were waiting for him.

PC Thomas waved goodbye to him and kept on walking in the other direction.

Jack made it to the woodland area and told the boys about his encounter with the policeman. Although he tried to make out that he had it all under control and it was no big deal, the others did look a bit uneasy, as the exhilaration of their plundering had died down and they now considered they might get caught.

Jack tried to change the subject and said, "Let's just get on with it, shall we?"

They looked around to see that no one was around watching them and went into the area where they had hidden the bike. It was under a pile of branches and looked like it was untouched.

"It's still locked," Greg cried.

"Oh yeah, we were meant to fix that, weren't we?" Jack mumbled.

"It would be a lot quicker if we could ride the bike out of here instead of carrying it," said Jacob. "That way, it would also look less suspicious if PC Thomas saw us."

The others agreed but they hadn't brought anything with which to cut the bicycle lock open. Jack checked his pockets and found a pocket knife his dad had given him. It was a Swiss army knife that had loads of gadgets on it, and Jack had loved it when he got it for Christmas. Apparently, it was something his grandad had passed down as some sort of heirloom. He wasn't usually allowed to use it at home, but tonight he had thought it might be handy to keep it on him just in case.

"I've got a knife," Jack said.

He went up to the bike and started sawing on the plastic cable-tie that was wrapped around the wheels. Fortunately, it didn't take too long for Jack to cut through it, and once it was free, they threw the plastic into the bushes and got the bike up.

"Maybe I'll just ride it home, shall I?" Jack looked around at the others, hoping they wouldn't see how eager he was at trying the mountain bike out. But the rest of the boys were happy for Jack to take it as they would prefer not to be caught with it if the police were looking for it, so they quickly agreed it was a good idea.

Jack couldn't wait to get it onto the road, although as he had never ridden a bike before, he didn't want to be seen wobbling in front of his friends. As he led the bicycle slowly down the street, he waved goodbye to the others. Once they were out of sight, he lifted his leg over and sat on the saddle.

Taking a deep breath, Jack put his feet on the pedals and pushed gently. At first he was quite shaky and had to put his feet down a few times. But then he came to a place where it was slightly downhill and he decided to go for it. Jack pushed the pedals and started going round and round with his legs, and the more speed he got, the steadier he became. Soon he had got the hang of it and he could feel the wind swooshing past his face; he loved the feeling of freedom that he got. Jack cycled all around town and felt properly happy, a feeling that had been unfamiliar to him for a long while.

Suddenly, as he was cycling past the church, he heard the bells chiming. It was 9 p.m.! Jack remembered the promise he had given to his mum and quickly cycled towards home. She would be worried and angry with him for being late, and the happy feeling rapidly disappeared. A sense of dread filled him instead, and as he approached his street, he screeched to a halt outside his house and moved the bike to his backyard. They didn't in truth have a shed, it was just a small area where they kept the bins, but he had to tell the boys something to convince them to let him keep the bike. Jack put it there and hid it behind some cardboard and the wheelie bins.

He opened the door slowly and walked inside. As he hung his coat up, his mum stormed towards him.

"Where have you been?! I thought I said no later than 8 p.m.? It is now past nine! If I can't trust you to keep to the rules of this house, then I won't be able to let you go out in the evenings." Jack's mum was fuming, much as Jack had expected.

He just looked down and said, "I'm sorry, Mum. We just lost track of time." At least that was a half-truth.

Jack didn't like disappointing his mother, but at the same time he was feeling angry. *Why do I always have to be told off? I'm surely old enough to look after myself now and really shouldn't have to keep to these stupid house rules. I can't wait for when I can move out and do whatever I want*, he thought.

When his mum had stopped ranting, he walked upstairs and went to his bedroom. Lying in bed, the teenager thought about his day. Thinking about that bike ride he had just had made him smile to himself; at least no one would be able to take that experience away from him.

3

A Mother's Worries

Mrs Sienna Hart sat down on the sofa with a thud. It was 9.30 p.m.; finally, she could catch her breath and have a moment of peace. She sipped her cup of tea slowly and started to wish that it was something stronger. As she lay down to rest her head, she closed her eyes and thought of the day's events. It was hard looking after four children all by herself. The youngest was only eighteen months and was still waking up in the night, so she knew that it wouldn't be long until that familiar cry would call out at her, demanding her attention and wanting to be soothed back to sleep, unable to do it himself. The twins Ella and Jane had been a shock, and those first few years had been exhausting, but at least she had had a husband to help.

For nine years it had just been the three of them: Simon, her and Jack. The couple had not thought they would have more children after Jack, because although they had tried for a few years, nothing had happened, so they had become content with what they had and were settled. It was when Sienna turned thirty-six that she had had a sudden urge to try again, and then the twins came.

Only a few years later Charlie was born and their lives were changed forever.

They were happy nonetheless, even when things were chaotic and children everywhere, it seemed. Sienna had always prided herself on being a good mum and devoted her life to her children. After the twins she gave up her job as a nurse and was a stay-at-home mum. That was all fine, as they could manage on Simon's salary. She knew they had an old-fashioned lifestyle – her husband working and coming home to a homecooked meal, then spending the evening with his feet up watching football, while she cared for the home and the children, fussing over him and making sure he was looked after. She didn't mind much that she had the main burden of the household. She was the mum, after all, and took the responsibility with pride. Being a mother was her job, even though she had friends who tried to tell her that "these days men should pull their weight at home as well" and some asked if she did not miss going out to work. Of course, she had days when she felt like just leaving the house and being by herself for a day or even just a few hours, but she soon overcame those feelings. A bar of chocolate and five minutes alone in the bathroom was enough to bring her back to reality.

But when Simon died so suddenly in the car crash, it changed everything. The whole happy life balance was shattered in a day, and she had to rebuild her life from scratch. They hadn't got round to arranging life insurance; why would they? It didn't feel like a priority at the time, and now she certainly wished she had. Sienna was forced to go back to work and, luckily, her mum was able to help with the kids. It was almost impossible to manage everything with school runs, food shops and cleaning, and still she was only just about able to pay the bills.

She was worried about Jack but didn't readily know what to do. He had always been her special boy, and they would have story times and cuddle up to watch a movie every Friday when he was little. Their bond had been strong, but when the twins and Charlie came along, she could feel how she was getting stretched with her attention. The little ones demanded so much of her, and she knew that with Jack being older, he could look after himself. Sienna had started to rely on him as she had done her husband. Even though he was only fourteen, there had been a lot of responsibility put on him with babysitting and general jobs around the house. She had noticed him slipping away from her. Her cuddly little boy was no more, and she was lucky to get a smile out of him these days, never mind a hug.

She felt helpless, as it was always Simon who had been the one who was good at talking to Jack. When Jack became a teenager, they had gone on a camping trip and they had come back smiling, and Sienna knew they had had a good father-son time. Oh, how she missed those days! Now Jack was out past his curfew and didn't even seem that sorry about it. The head teacher had been in touch on several occasions saying that Jack had been sent to detention, and when Sienna had confronted him about it, he had just shrugged his shoulders and said he didn't want to talk about it. However much she loved him, her ability to help and worry about him was limited. She had so much else to worry about, that worrying about Jack was just put to one side, and she tried to think this was just a phase he was going through. All teenagers were grumpy and spent all their time in their rooms. To be honest, at times when he went out with his friends, she felt relieved. At least he was entertaining himself and not there

Jack & DADS
CAMPING TRIP.

They had gone on a camping trip
and they had come back smiling.

to annoy his siblings. For some reason he always seemed to torment them one way or another, and it was something that had built up a wall between them, as Sienna had been protective of the babies and Jack was the one sent to his room. At least when he was out, there was one less conflict to handle. She knew deep down that it was terrible to feel that way but she couldn't help it. She could only pray that tomorrow would be a less burdensome day and that with time all would work out.

4

An Isolated Place

It was finally the weekend. Saturdays were a day to chill out and relax after a busy week. Jack used to try to go out with his friends as much as he could, and his mum didn't seem to mind.

"Jack, would you mind doing me a favour today?" his mum asked. "I need this letter posted; it's extremely important."

Jack was munching on some toast. "Yeah, sure, Mum," he said in between chews.

"Thanks. I'm taking the girls and Charlie to the park. Make sure you are back for tea at five, OK?"

Jack nodded and grabbed the letter and his bag and went out.

He stepped out of the house and went through the backyard. Then he suddenly remembered: *the bike!* He looked around and didn't see anyone coming. His mum was still upstairs sorting his siblings out. Jack quietly went to the bin area and pulled the bike out. He had waited for an opportunity to ride it again, so slowly and gently he led the bike down the path and crossed the road.

When there was no one in sight, Jack sat on the saddle with excitement and put his feet on the pedals. With a push from his right leg, he was off!

It was a warm day and the sun was shining. Jack loved feeling the soothing wind on his face and how his hair blew around. He laughed to himself as he went faster down the hill. Cycling was so much fun! He decided to ride to the outskirts of the town centre, near the lake where it was more remote. It was still early enough that he could go for a whizz and still be back in time to meet his friends.

Jack was cycling along and was near the edge of the woodland, on the way to the lake. He decided to stop for a moment and take in the view. It was so quiet; the only thing audible was the sound of some nearby birds cheeping, as if singing a happy song to each other. The park was an isolated place where he would often go when he wanted to be alone, as not many walked down this road.

Just as he got off the bicycle, he could hear the sound of people approaching. Suddenly he was worried it might be PC Thomas or, even worse, Old Man Sam himself, who might recognise his bike. He looked around and couldn't see anyone so he cycled on. *Maybe I just imagined it,* he thought, but then, without any warning, three boys came running towards him from behind some rhododendron bushes and attacked him down to the ground!

As he hit the gravelly surface with extreme force, intense pain shot through his left foot as it landed awkwardly, and he cried out. It all happened so fast that Jack had no chance to defend himself. The boys kicked and punched him repeatedly and held him down.

Jack tried to call for help, but his voice was getting smaller and could barely be heard as he was seeing stars in front of his eyes. "Why are you doing this? I haven't got any money," Jack tried to reason with his attackers. Then he saw Ralph come up to him.

"Hello, Jack, thanks very much for this bike. It looks like a real nice one too! Kane will be pleased. What a steal!" Ralph burst out laughing hysterically, and so did his gang members.

Jack was in shock. He couldn't believe it; his chance of impressing Kane was gone, and Ralph obviously had been offered the same dare and decided to steal his bike, which was in fact not even his.

"Finish him," Ralph said.

One of the boys gave Jack a strong punch in the head and then they ran off.

When Jack woke up, he wasn't sure how long he had been unconscious. His head was pounding like a drum, and everything he looked at seemed a bit blurry. The attempt to try to look around to see if anyone else was about was incredibly painful, and he could barely move. His body was so sore, and he struggled even to lift his arms.

Suddenly, Jack remembered his bag and the crucial letter his mum had asked him to post. It wasn't on his back! Frantically he tried to reach around to see where it had gone. He screamed out in pain every time he had to move, but he wanted to pull himself a bit nearer to the path. It might also be a good idea to be more visible so that, hopefully, someone who came past would be able to see him. The bag was still nowhere to be seen until... he saw a glimpse of it in the bush. A rustling noise came from

Jack tried to call for help, but his voice was getting smaller and could barely be heard as he was seeing stars in front of his eyes.

it and Jack froze. There might be wild animals about, and he wasn't in a position to run if there were.

The leaves moved and the bit of the bag he had seen disappeared. Then a moment later a fox came out. It had the bag in its mouth and looked straight at Jack. Jack was horrified and terrified at the same time. Did foxes attack humans? He couldn't remember and was trying to think back to any biology lessons he might have had. The best idea seemed to be to stay completely still; Jack held his breath, trying not to make a noise. The orange-coloured fox stood and stared for what seemed like an eternity, but then, with the bag still in its mouth, it ran off into the woods.

Jack dropped his head back onto the ground with a thump. Tears started streaming down his face. His backpack had his lunch, his best trainers and, of course, the all-important letter. How was he going to explain this to his mother? She would never forgive him. The pain was still extraordinarily intense, when all of a sudden voices could be heard. Jack quickly wiped his tears and tried to shout for help. His voice had nearly gone, so it wasn't a loud cry, but he attempted to shout the best he could.

"Help! Is there someone there?"

The voice was coming closer. It was a man talking on his phone. "Yes, I understand. I will be there in five minutes; I'm on my way."

Jack thought the voice sounded familiar. As the man walked past, he recognised him; it was Mr Ross! *That's even better;* surely, his teacher would help him.

"Mr Ross, it's me, Jack Hart!" he shouted with a croaky voice.

Mr Ross walked past with quick steps, seemingly in a hurry. He glanced towards the path where Jack was lying down.

Oh no, not Jack, he thought. *He's a troublemaker at the best of times. I certainly don't have time to mess about with helping him. Who knows, it might even be a trick for one his pranks. I bet the rest of his mates are hiding somewhere, ready to jump me and steal my wallet if I go anywhere near to help him. I won't fall for that; not a chance.* Mr Ross started to jog, trying to look like he hadn't seen him, and left Jack behind.

He was out of sight, and Jack was left alone again. Jack couldn't understand why his teacher had not helped him. Wasn't that something teachers had an obligation to do? Once again he felt his head fall back towards the ground. Everything went black.

5

Mr Ross' True Colours

Mr Daniel Ross was running late for his meeting with some of the other teachers from school. They were gathering together for a monthly Saturday brunch at the local café, which made amazing full English breakfasts, and Mr Ross was already salivating, thinking of the sausages and hash browns. As he walked into the restaurant, he spotted the others sat at the back and he gave them a little wave. The teacher hurried along and offered an apology for being slightly late: "So sorry I'm late, guys; I was just so busy doing a morning workout that I lost track of time." He wiped his brow a bit to show that he was slightly sweaty to add to the effect of his morning efforts. When no one seemed suitably impressed, he instead sat down and perused the menu. He already knew what he wanted but, not wanting to seem too eager, Mr Ross looked like he was still choosing and did the appropriate 'oohs' and 'aahs' over all the delicious choices. Once a few had gone up to order, Daniel joined the queue as well.

When they sat back down, Mr Ross made sure he sat opposite Miss Amelia Bell. She was the art teacher and was very pretty; she always had a smile on her face. She was chatting to Miss Chang about their holiday plans, and Mr Ross was intently trying to get in on the conversation. He leaned in and looked at each person as they spoke, making some nods and smiles as appropriate. The ladies didn't seem to be noticing Mr Ross until they paused in their conversation and he blurted out, "What about those kids in class 10A, eh? Quite a handful, aren't they?"

Miss Bell looked a bit perplexed over this sudden outburst but, being polite, she smiled and said, "Do you mean Jack Hart? I suppose he can be difficult, but I'm sure he could do quite well if he just had the opportunity."

Mr Ross was so pleased to get the attention of the lovely Miss Bell finally, so he did his best to keep the conversation going. "Ah yes, young Mr Hart. He is an enigma, that one. I just wish there was a way to reach him, you know? My passion is, of course, to help all these youngsters get the best out of life, which of course I'm sure is yours too – I mean, all of us here as educators." Mr Ross mumbled towards the end. "But if I could just reach him with some guidance, I'm certain I could get through to him. You know, I think he could just do with a male role model to show him the way in life. Poor thing lost his dad last year; I'm sure you remember that... Sad, sad times..." Mr Ross started to look into the middle distance for a moment and then inhaled sharply and looked back at Miss Bell with a concerned expression.

"But I suppose as teachers we only have so much time with them to make a real difference. Of course, if he would just pay more attention in class, I'm sure I would be able to truly hone him and make him into the man he so has the potential to be."

Miss Amelia Bell was the art teacher and was very pretty;
she always had a smile on her face.

Mr Ross was looking very pleased with himself and at the same time shaking his head at this impossible task. Miss Bell, who had been quiet up until now, suddenly looked at Mr Ross seriously.

"Do you genuinely mean that? That you want to make a difference to these kids?"

Mr Ross, a bit startled at Miss Bell's question, said with emphasis, "Why, yes, of course. After all, that is the reason I chose this profession – to become a leader and show the way to those who are lost." He held his fist in the air as a sign of victory, already imagining receiving a 'teacher of the year' award with all the staff and students of the school applauding him and patting him on the back. He would of course show suitable humility and look completely shocked, clutching his heart as if to say that he couldn't believe they had chosen him. In his 'thank you' speech he would say, "I never expected this; thank you so much. Of course, it has always been about the children…"

Mr Ross was suddenly woken from his daydream.

"Daniel?" Miss Bell was trying to get his attention.

"Oh, sorry, Amelia. I was just thinking of something. What did you say?"

She shuffled on her chair and leaned forward. "I was just saying that if you truly want to make a difference, you should come down to the youth club tonight. They meet at St Mark's church at 7 p.m., and any young people with problems either at home or with schoolwork can come down to get help. Some come down just to chill out and get a break from their home life. It would be great to have someone with your skills and leadership talents to be there – you know, to help guide them."

The slightly sarcastic tone was lost on Mr Ross, who nodded agreeably. Although he had a sense of panic at the thought of spending his Saturday night helping a bunch of teenagers, he could not let Miss Bell know that, so he showed eager interest and asked further questions about it. Finally, he said, "So will you be there, Amelia?"

She smiled and said, "Of course. I volunteer there every week as I am a member of the church."

Mr Ross looked delighted and went on to share his experience of church and how he was probably going to be appointed the leader there soon. It was just a matter of time.

At 7 p.m. exactly Mr Ross arrived at St Mark's church. For a moment he worried that Miss Bell might not actually be there but then shrugged it off and walked with determined steps towards the front door. He was met by a friendly guy who introduced himself as Jeff.

"Hello, you must be Amelia's friend. Welcome!" He had a broad smile and shook Mr Ross' hand vigorously.

Mr Ross nodded, said thank you and walked into the room. There were lots of activities set out: table tennis tables; a pool table; a café area with beanbags; and another area ready for any homework help that might be needed. He spotted Miss Bell in the café and walked towards her.

She waved at him and handed him a cup of tea. "You came!"

Slightly offended that she thought he might not, Mr Ross guffawed and said, "Of course! You can always count on me!" With a cheesy grin he scanned the room to get an idea of what he could expect from the evening.

"They should all be turning up soon. We get about twenty kids each week so should hopefully get a decent turnout. Would you mind helping out in the homework area? Lots of kids struggle with English."

Miss Bell continued folding napkins and getting hot drinks ready, and Mr Ross ambled around the room reading the notices on the wall, feeling ever so slightly out of place.

About ten minutes later the room was starting to fill up with teenagers. Some Mr Ross recognised from school, others he hadn't seen before. They all seemed to know what they were doing and were given hugs and high fives by the staff who were there. Jeff was laughing and poking fun at some of them at the pool table, and they all seemed relaxed and were enjoying themselves. Mr Ross, keen to impress Miss Bell, went up to some of them in the café.

"Hey kids, how's it hanging?" His attempt at sounding cool fell flat, and the girls he had approached looked at him as though he were from outer space. Trying just to ignore him, they continued their conversation, and Mr Ross was left feeling awkward. For the rest of the evening he tried joining a few groups of kids and laughing when they laughed, although not properly following what they were talking about.

Most of them just ignored him, but one boy came up to him. "Hey, is it Mr Ross?"

Mr Ross was relieved to have someone come up to talk to him, and he quickly looked to see if Miss Bell was noticing his final success.

"Ah, Bobby, how nice to see you! Are you having a nice evening?" Mr Ross smiled towards him and put his hand patronisingly on his shoulder, attempting to be the guide he had come to be.

Bobby looked at Mr Ross' hand, then brushed it off and said, "I just wanted to ask you why you are so hard on us in English. I don't get all that grammar talk you go on about."

Mr Ross looked at him sternly. "Well, if you paid more attention to your books, maybe you *would* understand." He spoke quietly and through his teeth, but still smiling, which made it sound slightly threatening.

Bobby sighed and decided it wasn't worth the argument and walked off.

Mr Ross looked at Miss Bell, who was holding hands with a young man who also seemed to be a volunteer from the church. When he saw the guy kiss Miss Bell on the cheek, Mr Ross knew it was time to leave. "What a waste of an evening," he muttered to himself as he let himself out without even saying goodbye.

6

Could This Be It?

The sun was setting now, and it looked like it was past dinner time. Jack stirred again and tried to get a bit more comfortable but winced at the pain in his leg. He had lost track of time and how long he had been lying on this path. Every time he moved, the pain started again, and his head was particularly sore. He was drenched entirely from the cold sweat he was having, and although it had been a hot day, he was shivering from feeling cold.

It was typical that this had to happen in a quiet area where hardly anyone walked around. He hadn't seen anyone all day, apart from Mr Ross who had acted like he hadn't seen him. If only he had a phone to call an ambulance; but his mum had not been able to afford to give him one. Once again, he felt himself wishing that he had more money and was allowed to have what others seemed to count as basics.

As he was concentrating on breathing and trying to think what to do, the crunching noises of footsteps came closer. Then he could hear the sound of someone whistling and walking towards him. Finally, someone to help! Jack tried to sit up and gathered all his strength to call out for attention.

Just then a crackling noise from a walkie talkie came on. "PC Thomas, come in." The man stopped, picked up his radio and listened.

"Thomas here. Over."

"We have a burglary on Summerfield Road. It needs immediate backup. Over."

"I'll be right there. Over and out." The policeman put his radio back on his belt and started walking with a pace.

"Help!" cried Jack, and PC Thomas stopped for a moment in his tracks. He looked and saw that Jack was lying down behind the bushes. *It's that scoundrel, Jack Hart,* he thought. *I wonder what he is doing there. Never mind; I have more important business to tend to. I'm sure the next person coming along will help him.*

The sound of running on the gravel made Jack honestly give up hope. What should he do now? How long would he have to wait until someone would be willing to help him?

While lying there, thoughts about his behaviour and what he had done came to mind. He knew he wasn't a model child by any means or that there were many excuses for why he was acting out. Everything was just so unfair. *Life* was unfair. Why should he behave nicely when everyone else had a better experience of life than him? Anger bubbled up inside of him, and he could feel his chest tighten. *I wish my dad were here; then things would be better,* he thought. He hadn't thought of his dad for a long time, and this added to his upset. The anger was building up, and he beat his fist to the ground until his knuckles bled. He started crying again in both frustration and grief. Then the thought came to him that this might be it. What

A crackling noise from a walkie talkie came on.
"PC Thomas, come in."

if no one came to help him and he indeed died here? It felt like he might die. The pain had mostly gone now as long as he stayed still, but there was no way he could move. His foot was twisted in a way that did not look good. It was most likely broken.

Jack started to think about his dad and what he would have thought of him. He had been a good man who was a role model for Jack, and Jack had looked up to him. He always talked about doing the right thing, and there was no way he would be happy with the way things had turned out for his son. He had believed in God and was always talking about his faith.

As a child, Jack had gone along with it. He had gone to Sunday school and sung worship songs and tried his best to be a good boy. But as he got older, he decided that he didn't want to have to get up early on a Sunday morning to go to church. It was incredibly dull and reminded him too much of school, which he'd prefer not to have to do at the weekend. Jack would much rather lie in bed or hang out with his friends. His parents insisted he should go, but when he was twelve, they eventually said they didn't want to force him but instead that he should go because he wanted to. Jack was pleased with this and jumped at the chance to miss out on boring church. Since then he had given up any thoughts on God or that there is any higher purpose in life. When his dad died, that just reinforced his lack of faith further. What kind of good God would let a dad die like that and leave a whole family? It didn't make any sense and it wasn't fair.

But as he was lying there, death did come more to mind and what would happen to him if he did die. Could he genuinely be sure that there would be nothing? What if he was wrong and there was a God, and because of what he had done, he would go to hell?! The thought made him shudder. There was also another thing that bothered him: if there was no God, which he had chosen to believe, were we just here on earth for no other reason than to eat, work, sleep, then die? It wasn't often he reflected on these things, but as he lay there, lots of thoughts were swimming through his head.

He also considered his mum. She had indeed done everything she could to keep the family going and amazingly still kept her faith in God. Jack didn't understand it. How could she still believe that God existed? She said that God is in control and that he looks after us no matter what – even if things happen that we don't like. *Well, I'm not sure that's the kind of God I want to believe in,* Jack had thought. If you were to have a God, then surely the point would be to have a protector and someone who would make sure you were happy all the time, preferably one who also could make you rich and famous. In short, a genie would be handy.

Once again he tried to call for help. It seemed pointless, but as he had no other choice, he might as well give it a shot.

After a few minutes there was a noise again. Someone was walking past! The footsteps sounded slower, as if someone had difficulty walking. Raising his head, Jack tried to see who it was. As the person came nearer, he first saw the shoes. They were brown with laces and old-fashioned looking. The man also had a walking stick so he must be elderly. Maybe he would have some more compassion than his teacher and the policeman. Jack tried to use all his might to shout for help.

"Please help me! I'm injured!"

The man stopped and called back, "Who's there?"

Jack froze. A sinking feeling came into the pit of his belly. He recognised that voice and suddenly he knew that he was doomed forever. That was Old Man Sam, and there was not a chance that he would help him. Why would he? If Old Man Sam would find him, then he would probably phone the police, and there would be all sorts of trouble. Maybe he would just walk past like the others. The weary boy let his head fall back down to the ground and closed his eyes. If he had thought he might be dying earlier, he certainly wished it now.

7

Time to Confess

The old man stopped in his tracks as he thought he had heard a noise behind the bushes. As he moved closer towards it, he could see a teenage boy lying on the ground, seemingly injured. Slowly he approached him to assess what had happened. Then he recognised him. Sam saw that it was Jack whom he had known from walking past his house frequently and who had been actively harassing him. The boy was known to get into trouble and clearly hated the elderly man. Sam gazed at him now, with blood on the ground and his leg obviously wounded. He considered his options and then pulled out his mobile phone from his pocket. After he had spoken to the emergency services and knew they were on their way, he bent down next to Jack, who was either asleep or unconscious. Sam used his handkerchief to wipe off the blood and sweat from his forehead and got a water bottle to offer him a sip if his mouth was dry. He saw that the boy was shivering so he took off his coat and laid it on him to keep him warm. The old man stayed and spoke comforting words until the paramedics arrived and took care of the rest. When he knew that Jack would be suitably cared for, he slipped away unnoticed.

Jack woke up in a daze and wasn't sure where he was. He could hear sirens and people talking around him. "You'll be alright, son. We are taking you to the hospital now. You are very fortunate that you were found as this leg will need some medical attention," a voice was saying. Jack tried to open his eyes but he was feeling so tired. All he could do was stay still and feel how he was being lifted onto a stretcher and into what he imagined was an ambulance. He looked down and noticed there was a coat on him that he didn't recognise. It had a musty smell of old spice, but the warmth was making him feel more relaxed so he lay back and felt his muscles lose their tension. Somebody was asking him questions, but he couldn't muster the strength to answer. He saw one of the paramedics was looking at his leg and had a concerned look on his face, but then smiled at him reassuringly and said it would all be fine.

Once they arrived at the hospital, Jack was wheeled into the accident and emergency department. He seemed to have priority and was taken through to see a doctor almost straight away.

"This boy here is about fourteen years old and was found by Mr Green by the roadside. He has a head wound, most likely a fractured leg, and cuts and bruises. He is also quite dehydrated. The family has been informed." The paramedic was passing on the information to the doctor on call.

Jack listened intently to what they were saying. *The family has been informed!* So his mum might be on her way down to find him. Suddenly, he had an intense

Once they arrived at the hospital, Jack was wheeled into the accident and emergency department.

longing for his mum. All he wanted was for her to sit with him and say everything was going to be OK, and hopefully she wouldn't be too mad with him.

Jack was given some fluids on a drip, and after he had gone through the process of getting his leg X-rayed, he finally was taken to a ward to wait for the next thing to happen. He was just trying to get comfy when he saw someone walking past his curtain partition.

"Mum?" he called out.

Jack's mum turned around and came towards him, pulling the curtain back dramatically. "Oh, there you are!" She had tears in her eyes and gave him a big hug and a kiss. "I have been so worried about you. When Niall came round to ask for you, I was surprised that you hadn't met with them and no one had seen you all day. Then, thank goodness, Mr Green found you and he phoned me straight away." She tried to smile as if she didn't know whether to laugh or cry. "So, the doctor says you will be alright; you have a broken leg, but it's not a bad break so they will give you a proper cast tomorrow. Your head seems OK, but they will have to look out for any signs of a concussion and so will keep you here overnight. What on earth happened to you?" She looked at Jack with genuine concern and was waiting eagerly for an answer from her son.

"Well, I..." Jack didn't know how to reply. He was just about to open his mouth to say something when he was interrupted by another visitor.

It was PC Thomas! Jack felt a cold shiver go down his spine. Maybe this was it; he was finally going to get done for stealing the bike. Old Man Sam must have known it was him and had grassed on him yet again. Jack looked down to avoid any eye contact with the policeman.

"Oh, PC Thomas, thank you for coming!" Jack's mum smiled at the copper.

"Yes, well, we got a call that there could have been some foul play going on here and just needed to get a statement from the boy." He seemed a little uneasy, and his posh English accent seemed more evident than usual; he also avoided looking Jack in the eye.

"Foul play? Jack, please tell me what happened!" She looked even more concerned now, so Jack would have to tell her something, but there was no way he could say he had been beaten up by Ralph and his friends. If they found out he had snitched, they would never let him forget it. There was no way he wanted to get beaten up again. But he did know he had to tell his mum *something*.

"Yes... well... it's silly, really... I was just going for a stroll down towards the lake, and then I thought I would climb a tree and see how high I could go. But then I lost my footing and fell. I must have broken my leg and hit my head from the fall. There was no foul play though. Promise."

Jack's mum looked relieved but gave him a bit of a scolding. "You stupid boy! What are you doing climbing trees at your age anyway?" Turning towards PC Thomas, she said, "Why did you think there was foul play, PC Thomas?"

The policeman looked suspiciously at Jack and didn't seem convinced by his story. Then he looked at Jack's mother and said slowly, "Hmm... Well, it was just something Mr Green said when he found the boy. He said it looked like he had been beaten up... but if Jack says he fell out of a tree..."

Jack looked nervously at his hands and hoped the policeman would believe his story even though it wasn't a great one. Luckily, his mum saved him.

"Well, I believe Jack, so if that's what he says happened, then that is what happened. Thank you for stopping by though."

PC Thomas grunted a sort of acknowledgement and then left them.

"Would you like something to eat? Let me go and see what snacks they have in the cafeteria." Jack's mum went off in search of food and left Jack alone with his thoughts.

He had got away with it once again. No one knew about the stolen bike or that he had been beaten up by Ralph. He was in the clear. But why did he still have that feeling deep down that, in truth, he wasn't?

8

Law Over Kindness

PC Thomas arrived at the police station late. He was on the night shift, and it had already been a busy night with a burgled house, a call out for domestic violence and then the discovery of Jack Hart. The policeman put his keys on the table and sat down with a loud sigh. His desk was covered with all the paperwork. The workload made him feel a moment of despair at all the administration he had to do. In his pile were different reports, from shoplifting offences to drink driving in the area, as well as the online ones posted on the system. Most of them were young offenders, some even as young as twelve. PC Thomas had only been a policeman for five years, but he had seen enough to know that when they started that young in the life of crime, they rarely changed. He thought about the number of times he had spoken to them when they were caught – they would show remorse, pleading with him, saying they would never do it again and that this was their first time – only to see them again the following month arrested for a similar crime, this time looking sheepish but not as remorseful as they had been the first time around. *Some people just can't change,* PC Thomas had decided.

He hadn't always been this cynical. When he had started at the college of policing, he had had aspirations and real hope that he could uphold the law in the community and improve people's lives. He had an extreme need to follow the set guidelines. Ever since he was little and playing board games with his family, he would intently study the rule book before the game started, and should anyone deviate from the regulations, he was there to shout at them their mistake. PC Thomas thought back to when in school he was always chosen to be the class representative for the school council. He was there ready to put things right and genuinely believed that people who didn't obey the rules should be punished. Without order in the world, there would be utter chaos, and that would just be a terrible world to live in. No, the law was the law, and if it wasn't followed, there should be consequences.

PC Thomas had believed in rehabilitation when he first started. Everyone should be given the benefit of the doubt, he had been told to think. In the beginning he thought there might be some truth to it, although he had had some misgivings. Then he met Arnold. Arnold was a repeat offender who had done some truly terrible things. Every time he was brought into the station, he looked at the police with intense evil in his eyes. The criminal showed a deep disdain for the force that made even the bravest policeman shudder. Arnold had started when he was young; at only ten he had been delivering drugs for his big brother and his gang. From one petty crime to another it escalated, and once he became an adult, he didn't even seem to care anymore. Although he was given prison sentences, Arnold just went straight back to his criminal buddies when released and planned the next heist or assault.

PC Thomas could not even fathom the amount of disregard Arnold had for the law. It was beyond him, who saw the law as the pinnacle of society, the thing that made the world go round. His dealings with Arnold made him truly believe that once a criminal, always a criminal. He started to build up hate towards any person who committed a crime and saw them as lesser people. He probably didn't even notice the change or when it happened, but slowly, and with time, his heart had hardened and his compassion lessened by the day. It just made his quest to find and get these criminals arrested more intense, and it became an obsession that was starting to take over his whole identity. He rarely saw his family or had many friends, and he spent his free time still going over evidence or taking on extra shifts at work. He had tried to get a promotion to become a sergeant a few times but had been denied as was told he wasn't ready yet. Thomas couldn't understand it; if anyone would deserve to move up the ranks, it would be him. He would show them... All he needed was a case that no one else could solve; then maybe, just maybe, they would take him seriously.

Police Constable Thomas looked again at his pile of reports and to-do list. The list included writing up the dealings with Jack Hart that night. He was meant to write down his statement of events and Jack's supposed falling out of a tree. He knew as soon as he heard it that it sounded ludicrous. Teenagers don't usually climb trees, and especially Jack. He had had enough dealings with him in the past to know that he was almost certainly a rotten egg. Everything about him screamed 'criminal', and there was only one future for him: prison. The only question was what level of security he was going to end up in, but PC Thomas was sure that Jack was destined for a life behind bars.

As he was about to get the report started, he stopped for a moment. There was something about Jack's story that just didn't make sense. He read the online report from the paramedics and the police who had been at the scene. There were some photographs uploaded on the system, and he started to study them carefully. From one picture he could see that the nearest tree was at least two metres away. Looking at the photograph, it didn't look like the kind that you could climb, and it seemed unlikely that the boy could have fallen that far away from the actual tree. The only way he could know for sure would be to have a look at the scene for himself.

Once PC Thomas arrived at the site where Jack had been found, he got an uneasy feeling, as he recognised it as the place where he had spotted Jack in the woods and decided to leave him. His sense of duty gave him a certain pang of guilt, but he ignored it, telling himself that he wasn't to know and, as far as he remembered, it didn't look like Jack was in any trouble. That cleared his conscience for the time being.

The policeman examined the ground and could see the blood splatter from where Jack had fallen and hit his head. He looked up at the trees nearby and judged their distance to be eight metres, so even further than it had looked on the photos. There was no way Jack had fallen out of a tree to receive those injuries.

PC Thomas scoured the area further and found a backpack that was slightly torn. He saw that it was labelled 'Jack Hart'. Then just as he was about to leave,

PC Thomas scoured the area further and found a backpack that was slightly torn. He saw that it was labelled 'Jack Hart'.

he spotted something else on the other side of the path. To be sure of what he was seeing, the police constable went down close and shone his torch at it. As he examined it, he was more and more convinced. They were bicycle tracks and they led to where Jack had been found injured. He knew that Jack Hart did not own a bike. A sudden thought occurred to him. Could it be possible that Jack had stolen Sam Green's bicycle? It was the only bike reported stolen in the past month. It couldn't just be a coincidence.

PC Thomas smiled a broad, knowing smile. *Oh, little Jack Hart, I knew you were guilty...* He took some pictures on his phone as evidence and then returned to the police station. The boy could have a night of peace, but tomorrow judgement would come. And PC Thomas loved judgement more than anything.

9

A Surprise Visitor

The next morning Jack woke up feeling sore, but at least he was safe. He was looking forward to going home and he couldn't believe his luck that he had managed to get the police off his back and his mum hadn't been angry with him either. Jack was a bit disappointed about losing the bike but he supposed that it wouldn't have lasted anyway. Hopefully, Ralph would leave him alone, as Jack hadn't ratted him out and also Ralph did get the bike, which presumably was what he wanted. Life would return to normal, and Jack could carry on with The Reds.

Although things seemingly had all worked out for Jack, he couldn't help feeling inexplicably sad. As he was sat there, he could feel his eyes getting watery, and there was a heaviness in his chest that was stronger than usual. He tried to distract himself by turning the TV on, but when the only programmes were the news and a nature documentary, he turned it off again and closed his eyes to rest for a while.

A nurse came in and told him he had a visitor.

"Oh, who is it?" Jack was hoping it was one of his friends from school.

"It's a lovely old man. Maybe he is your grand-father?" the kind nurse said. Jack looked at her in shock. Both his grandfathers had died when he was little, so if it wasn't them, there was only one other elderly man he could think of. But surely the old fogey wouldn't come to the hospital... There was no way that he would bother coming over to see him unless he had figured out that Jack had stolen the bike and was going to tell him what a useless lowlife he was and that he would report him to the police immediately.

Suddenly, Jack panicked. He didn't want to have this conversation and did not want to see Old Man Sam under any circumstances. He started to wail and scream that his leg was hurting really badly. The nurse looked worried and asked him where it was hurting, and when Jack continued screaming in pain, she went to get some more painkillers. Jack was panting hard in between his outcries and faintly asked the nurse, "Please could you tell the old man that I'm not feeling well and would prefer not to have any visitors right now?" The nurse nodded under-standingly and went behind the curtain to give the guest the news.

Jack could hear them, as there was only a piece of fabric between them. "Maybe, try again later?" the nurse said apologetically.

"Oh, I am so sad to hear that he is hurting. Yes, I will come and see him another time."

Jack recognised Old Sam's voice and bit his lip at the thought of him coming back. Hopefully, his mum would arrive soon and he could be discharged and go home before the old man returned.

"But would you please just give him this? It's what I came to drop off, really. Many thanks."

Sam left and the nurse came back with both the medications and the gift for Jack. She smiled at him and handed him the lovely wrapped box. "He must care for you a lot. Such a lovely man." The nurse continued measuring out the painkillers and then left Jack to it.

Jack didn't want a gift from Old Man Sam. What was he doing giving him a gift? All they had done was torment him for months, and now Jack was getting a present... It didn't make sense. The box sat on Jack's bedside table, taunting him. It was a beautiful box with a big ribbon tied around it. In fact, Jack couldn't remember when he last had been given a fantastic gift like that. But he still refused to open it. The flustered boy couldn't bear to look at it anymore so he shoved it on the floor. He closed his eyes and tried to go to sleep.

Jack woke up with a jolt. He had had a bad dream and at first he was a bit confused about where he was. As he was getting his bearings, he remembered that he was in the hospital and that he had a broken leg and possible concussion. Suddenly, his mum appeared from behind the curtain and she was looking happy.

"Good news!" she said. "The doctor said he doesn't think you have a concussion and that you are free to come home." She was so pleased to be able to take her boy home that she started collecting his things immediately and arranged with a nurse to get a wheelchair to take him to the car.

Jack was relieved too. It would be good to get out of the hospital and even better if they could get out before Old Man Sam came back.

Just as they were heading for the lift, one of the nurses called after them, "Wait! You forgot this." She handed over the gift from Sam to Jack. "You must have dropped it under the bed. Good job I managed to get to you before you left!" The kind lady smiled and wished them a safe journey home.

Jack's mum asked about the gift, and Jack mumbled something about an old man having given it to him.

"Oh, it must have been Sam! It's amazing that he found you, you know. When he phoned me last night, he told me all about him walking down that road yesterday. He never walks on that side of town, but for some strange reason, he had a strong urge that he should go there at that time. When he found you, he just knew that that was why he was meant to go that way. Quite a miracle, if you think about it."

Jack didn't answer. It was all just getting a bit too much. Old Man Sam thought it was a miracle that he found him half-dead on the road so that he could save him? Jack, the one who had called him names, threw eggs on his house and generally hated him... Why? What was going on? Not only that but he also came around and gave him a present!

Jack stayed silent for the rest of the journey and didn't know what to think or to feel. He would never do what Old Man Sam had done. No way would he, say, go and give Ralph a present after he had beaten him up. Who does that? If anything, he would have planned his revenge. It had crossed his mind that he should get the gang together to arrange some kind of payback on those guys but at the same time he was scared of what they might do back again. Maybe they just needed to wait a bit until they weren't expecting it.

Back at home his sisters ran up to hug him. For once Jack didn't roll his eyes at them or tell them to buzz off.

He was, in fact, pleased to see them and returned their hugs. His mum kept checking in on him, giving him snacks and fluffing his pillow. He was really enjoying the attention, and it reminded him of how he used to feel as a young boy. Later on, in his bedroom, he lay down to have a little rest and listen to some music. Then he noticed on his bedside table the gift from Old Man Sam. His mum must have put it there when they came home from the hospital. Jack looked at it again, and the feeling of guilt and being undeserving came back. Finally, he decided it wouldn't hurt to find out what was in the box. If it was rubbish then maybe he could throw it away, and it would make him feel better knowing it was a useless present. It would probably be something stupid like a trophy or something little children liked to collect.

Slowly he unwrapped the bow. His hands were shaking slightly, and he tried to steady himself as he was ripping the paper off. Once he had removed the paper and the bow, he saw that there was a small box inside. Carefully he lifted the lid to see what was inside it. There he found a key. *Strange,* thought Jack. *I wonder what it is for.* He lifted the key, and at the bottom of the box there was a note. It said:

Dear Jack,

I know how much you would like a bike of your own, so here is a key to a secure lock that goes to a bike that is parked in your backyard. I hope you will enjoy it – once your leg has healed of course!

Much love,

Sam

Carefully, he lifted the lid to see what was inside it.
There he found a key.

Suddenly, the paper was getting wet. Jack noticed that tears had started rolling down his cheeks.

10

The Moment of Truth

PC Thomas was excited. He had spent all day matching the tyre tracks that he had discovered where Jack had been found with the type of tyre that had been on Sam Green's missing bike. Once he had worked out the model and brand, he was a hundred percent certain that they were both the same. Although his supervisor had said it was a bit circumstantial and not enough proof that Jack had stolen the bike, in PC Thomas' mind, and according to his instincts, it was more or less a case solved. To ease his boss, all he needed was a confession from the boy and then that was it, Jack would go on the record as a juvenile delinquent. Oh, the joy of solving another mystery – but, more than that, getting another criminal to justice! Following the law was what he lived for, what kept him going day after day without fail.

With determined strides he walked up to the Hart household. He rapped the door knocker firmly so that there would be no question that someone was at the door.

After a few seconds the door opened and Mrs Hart appeared behind it. "Oh, hello, PC Thomas. Can I help you?" Her voice was steely, as their last encounter hadn't been completely friendly with him accusing her son of doing something unlawful.

The policeman knew he had to tread lightly to be able to go in and get the confession from Jack. "Good morning, Mrs Hart. Nothing to worry about. I only wanted to check on Jack and simply ask him a question or two – just to complete my report, you see." He tried to look relaxed, and smiled, but he was eager to get in and get the truth out in the open.

"Well, I'm not sure now is the best time... Jack is resting."

PC Thomas was getting fidgety. He knew he needed to get this confession soon or else lawyers might get involved, and then there would be no chance of getting the truth as they had a standard answer of "no comment" to everything. His best bet was to have a casual chat, and if the boy just so happened to admit that he had stolen the bike, then of course it would be his duty as a police constable to report it.

"It really won't be long, I promise. It's just I am overloaded with work and I simply can't come back later as this is the time I have allocated for this case." He started to walk in through the door, and Mrs Hart didn't have the chance to stop him as he pushed past her. "Jack, PC Thomas here. Just wanting to say hello." The policeman searched in each room as he walked through the house. He found Jack in the living room with his leg raised, eating a piece of toast.

Jack looked shocked at seeing PC Thomas and nearly dropped his toast on the floor. His mother came in after him and looked most displeased.

"If you don't mind, could I please have a moment alone with Jack. Just need to check over his story again.

Won't take a minute." Thomas looked at Mrs Hart, waiting for her to leave the room.

She stood defiantly for a moment and said, "I think I should be here for this. Just in case there is something I need to know." She sat down, and Thomas knew it was probably best that Jack had a guardian present and only hoped it wouldn't ruin the chances of getting a confession from him.

"So, Jacky boy, how's the leg?" Although he was asking a caring question, there was no sign of any concern or care in his eyes; in fact, his eyes were boring into Jack's with such intensity, Jack had to look away.

"Fine, I guess," Jack said quietly.

"Yes, well, that's good, isn't it? The thing is, I have come over here as I just have some little questions about your story about you falling out of a tree to receive these injuries. Something doesn't quite add up." PC Thomas stopped for effect and looked at Jack to see how he might react.

Jack swallowed hard and didn't dare say anything, so the policeman continued.

"This was found at the scene – recognise it? It was all the way in the bushes, far away from where you supposedly landed." The policeman held up Jack's torn backpack that he had carried in a bag.

Jack gave a silent gulp.

"The thing is that the nearest tree is almost eight metres away from where you were found, so unless you were Superman who flew out of the tree and then crashed on the ground, it doesn't make mathematical sense that you could have fallen from a tree." Once again he paused to see if what he was saying would have an impact on the boy.

Jack still didn't say anything and was looking down on the floor to avoid his eye contact. PC Thomas was a bit disappointed that the boy hadn't crumbled under these revelations but took comfort in the silence as a sign of guilt.

"The other thing that was discovered was bicycle tyre marks that led up to the point where you were found. And it was the same tyre marks that matched the bicycle that was stolen from Mr Green just a few days ago!" His voice was spoken with extra volume to emphasise his point, and he was nearly breathless, looking at Jack with accusing eyes. "How do you explain that, Jack?" He was so desperate to get a confession that he was nearly shaking.

Jack looked scared and his bottom lip started to tremble. He didn't know what would be best: confess the truth or still stick with his lie? Everything was swimming around in his head, and the exhausted boy felt that he had finally had enough of lying. It was so tiring to keep track of what he had said and not said that he just wanted it to end. "I don't have it anymore," was all that he could say.

"Ah-ha! So you *did* steal the bike then!" PC Thomas was almost delirious at the results. He was right, and there was nothing that made him feel more exhilarated than being right.

Mrs Hart looked shocked and stared at Jack. "Is this really true?"

Jack slumped his shoulders and decided to tell the truth, even though it meant mentioning Ralph and the others. The admission could well be a death sentence, but maybe if he asked for them not to tell Ralph that he had told the police, he could get away with it.

Jack told PC Thomas everything, from Kane's dare, to hiding the bike in the woods, to being beaten up and left basically for dead. The copper had his tape recorder at the ready and greedily noted everything that Jack said. Once he had finished, Jack was exhausted but also relieved. This secret had been weighing on him more than he had known, and although he was worried about the consequences, telling the truth did make him feel better.

PC Thomas stood up and walked towards the door. "Thank you for your cooperation, Jack. I will be in touch once I have talked to Mr Green and found out how he wants to press charges. This misdemeanour will probably go on your record, so bear that in mind." With that, he left the house and half-skipped down to Mr Green's house. He couldn't wait to tell him the good news. This was turning into a fabulous day.

Later on in the afternoon there was another knock on the Harts' front door. Jack was sitting in his bedroom, thinking about what might happen to him, when his mum popped her head around the door. "There is someone here to see you, Jack," she said softly and then opened the door wider to let the visitor in.

Jack looked up to see Old Man Sam and looked hesitantly at him as he walked into the room. Jack's mum left them to it, and then it was just the two of them together.

"So, did you get my present?" Sam stood at the end of Jack's bed and looked at him with kind, smiling eyes.

Sam was acting confused, and Jack looked up at him and explained, "No, the bike is great. It's just... I don't deserve it." Saying it out loud gave Jack a lump in his throat, and he knew that it was true. After all that he had done to Sam and every kid he had bullied, he didn't deserve a bike – or any kind of kindness for that matter.

Jack looked up to see Old Man Sam and looked hesitantly at him as he walked into the room.

He deserved a punishment, which he was expecting from PC Thomas.

Jack looked at him, stunned for a moment, then said, "Um... yes, thank you so much... but I can't take it." He

"I see," said Sam knowingly. "You feel that because you stole my bike, I shouldn't reward you by giving you a new bike." He spoke softly and didn't seem to have any anger in his voice.

Jack looked amazed. "You knew it was me? And still you wanted to give me a gift?" He shook his head, not understanding. "Why? I have been horrible to you. Why would you still be kind to me? It makes no sense." His voice was wavering now. He could cope with being scolded by the policeman, but the kindness of this old man was more than he could handle.

"Well, I suppose when you are family, it's easy to forgive." Sam looked down at his shoes and then slowly glanced at Jack to see his reaction. Jack looked confused.

"What do you mean 'family'? I don't understand..."

"Yes, well this is hard for me to say, but the truth is that I am your grandfather."

Jack's mouth dropped open. "How is that possible? Why have you not said anything? Dad never spoke of you so I thought you were dead!" The questions were tumbling out of Jack like a waterfall.

Sam showed with his hands that Jack should slow down and that he would explain. "You see, the thing is that your father and I didn't exactly get along when he was younger. In fact, I think Simon hated me for the way I treated him. I wasn't the best dad and didn't know any better. I thought I was teaching him to be tough and a man by being hard on him. I also had times when I drank too much, and I deeply regret the things that happened then.

My wife left me and that made me take it out on your dad even more." Sam took a breath to steady his voice as he was starting to get emotional. "Simon did everything he could to avoid me when he was a teenager, and in a way it worked, us doing our own things and never speaking to each other. I was still hurting and didn't realise that your dad was slipping away from me. On his eighteenth birthday we had some cake and then he announced that he was moving out. Before I had the chance to ask any questions, he had packed his things and was out of the door. That was the last time I saw him."

Jack was still stunned and sat in amazement at what he was hearing. He had always imagined his dad as a hero, someone who never had done anything wrong. Hearing about his childhood like this was eye-opening. He was eager to hear more so asked Sam, "Well, how did you find out about us then?"

Sam shifted his position on the bed and looked at Jack. "When Simon left, I was heartbroken, but I told myself it was better this way and that he would have a chance for a happier life without me. I never tried to find him as I thought that he knew where I was and would look me up if he wanted to. I probably never would have known about you if it wasn't for something that happened to me that changed my life for ever."

Jack leaned forward and listened intently to his grandfather's story.

"I had been carrying on for years being miserable and lonely, but not doing anything about it. Things were getting hard, and I was starting to struggle to know what to do to make things better – although, just like you said now, I felt that I didn't deserve to have a better life. I had been such a terrible father that this depressing way of living was only a result of my bad behaviour. Happiness just wasn't an option for me.

"But then one day something changed. I was walking home from the pub and someone handed me a leaflet. At first I thought it was a fish and chip pamphlet and decided to check it out when I got home. However, when I read it later, it wasn't for food; it was advertising a meeting for that evening at a church called Smyrna Baptist. The leaflet read, 'Do you want to change your life for the better? Do you feel you don't deserve it and there is no hope? If you have answered yes to both those questions, then come down tonight!' I was stunned; this was exactly what I had been thinking and it stopped me in my tracks. A part of me wanted to just throw it out and see it as some crazy rallying from Christians who just wanted to prey on vulnerable people. Yet another part of me couldn't help wondering what it was exactly they were offering. In the end I decided I had nothing to lose. I could go down there and see what it was all about; if it was rubbish, no harm done, and if it worked, then added bonus.

"So I walked down to the church, and as I was standing outside, I started to have second thoughts. It felt so weird even thinking of going into a building like that. I hadn't been to a place like it since being a boy, when I was taken to Sunday school by my mum. I was nearly going to walk away, when the lady who was on the door called me over. She asked me if I would like to come in and started chatting to me and gave me a friendly smile. She was so nice that it made me feel at ease, and somehow I found myself walking inside – and before I knew it, I was sat at the back of the church. The room was quite full of people, and there was a band playing some music. I made sure to sit on the end of an aisle so that I could make a quick exit if it all went horribly wrong. Then the music really kicked up a notch, and people started standing up and waving their hands. There were words to the songs projected on the wall like they were in some sort of group karaoke night. It felt slightly odd watching them, but they all looked so happy. I was starting to feel jealous and couldn't understand what made them appear so at peace.

"I didn't know where to look or what to do, and just as I was thinking I might leave, the pastor stood up and started to speak. It felt rude to go then, so I stayed and listened. It wasn't that he said anything particularly special – in fact, I can't even remember what he was talking about – but there was something that I can't explain that happened to me. At the end of the meeting they said that anyone who wanted to be prayed for could stay behind, and I knew I had to do that. The pastor came to talk to me and then he prayed, and honestly, I felt like a new man. I know that is something people say, and believe you me, I was definitely suspicious when I had heard stories of conversions, but this was incredibly real. To know that God loved me and forgave me for the things I had done was such a relief, and I could feel guilt-free at last. From then on my life changed and I started making things better for myself and for others. Years later I decided to try and find my son, and it was difficult as I found out he had changed his last name to Hart instead of Green. I'm not sure why he did that; maybe he couldn't bear to have the same name as me. But with some help from a private investigator I found him here. I moved nearby but didn't have the courage to come and knock on your door. I thought he must hate me and wouldn't want me to find him. Then when I found out he had died, I was mortified that I never got a chance to ask for his forgiveness. It will be something I will regret until the day I die. I did look out for you though, and your friends, but for some reason you seemed to detest me."

Jack saw the hurt look on Sam's face and felt ashamed.

Sam paused for a moment as he let his story sink in for Jack, and he stood up and looked out of the window as if he was considering what to say next. He didn't know how Jack would react; he might think all of this a silly story and that he was just an old fool that he didn't want anything to do with.

Jack was quiet but then looked up at Sam and said, "Is it really possible to get that kind of forgiveness?"

Sam smiled and said, "Yes it is. That is, if you *want* to be forgiven. You see, forgiveness always works best when it is two ways. To forgive someone is important so that you don't become bitter and resentful, but to ask for forgiveness can be equally hard and needs to come from the heart for it to be worthwhile. That goes for people as well as with God." Sam sat down again at the end of Jack's bed and he looked nervously at his hands. There was always a chance that Jack didn't want his forgiveness, and he wasn't ready to face that possibility just yet.

Jack thought about what Sam had said and considered it carefully. Suddenly, he knew what it was he wanted most of all. The changed boy wanted his grandfather's forgiveness and he wanted to stop doing all the terrible things he had been doing. He even wanted God's forgiveness and prayed for it quietly. All of these thoughts came to mind in an instant like a lightning bolt, and as soon as it happened, that horribly niggly feeling he had been having in the pit of his stomach disappeared. He felt truly forgiven and that all that he had done before was gone and he could start over afresh. He touched Sam's hand gently and Sam looked up at him. "You know, Dad did become a Christian too and I'm sure he did forgive you." Jack inhaled sharply, holding his breath, and said, "Now it's my turn. Please forgive me, Grandad." Jack looked at him pleadingly, and Sam gave him a great smile and hugged him tightly as tears filled his eyes for a moment.

"Of course I will, son. *Of course I will.*"

Would you like to discuss this book with your friends or family?

Here's what you can do to get started.

- Pick the friends you would like to invite and have a chat with them about it.
- Choose a place you are going to meet up. It could be at one of your homes, for example, or in your church with your youth or Sunday school leader.
- Choose when and how often you are going to meet. Once a week usually works well or during your regular Sunday or mid-week meetings.
- Download the FREE questions sheet from **www.onwardsandupwards.org/product/jack-and-the-ultimate-dare**
- Read a chapter together each week, discuss the questions (and maybe add your own) and enjoy some snacks together!
- When you have finished the book, pick another one to go through together – maybe one of the books shown on page 84.

About the Author

Anita French was born in Exeter, England, however she is in fact half Swedish and half Italian. When she was six, her family moved to her mother's home country, Sweden, where she lived until her early twenties. In 2008 she got married and moved to Leeds, where her husband is from, and they have two children, Isobelle and Max. Anita studied English at university, which included educational studies and children's literature, and she is now working as a teaching assistant in Early Years in a primary school in Leeds. *Jack and the Ultimate Dare* was written as a way to make the parable of the Good Samaritan more accessible and relatable for children today, and to teach the valuable lessons of compassion, forgiveness and love. Anita has a desire to help children grow in their faith through her books, but also to think about the big questions in life and give opportunities to consider what the Bible teaches and how it fits with the present world we live in.

To contact the author, please write to:

anitafrench@live.com

Or visit the book's web page for more information:

www.onwardsandupwards.org/jack-and-the-ultimate-dare

Reviews

A story looking at current and relevant issues for the children today with the themes of The Good Samaritan woven into it. Some good lessons for everyone to learn in the plot.

Ruth Esplin
Head Teacher at a Church of England Primary School

This modern twist on the famous parable gets you involved from the beginning and makes you want to find out what happens to Jack. But get ready for the unexpected...

Kathy Owen
Primary School Teacher

A great story for 9-12s! Based on the Good Samaritan, a contemporary story that is fast-paced and engaging. I'll be using this in our Sunday School!

Matt Barrow
Children's Worker

Also from the Publisher

Get Over It
Fiona Linday
ISBN 978-0-9561037-7-2

Earlier that month, back home, I wasn't completely fazed when it dawned on me Mum couldn't make it. I should have known. Anyway, since then I agreed to come along and help my dad out. But I didn't want to come. I was doing him a favour, although why I should, I really don't know. After all, he's never done anything for me. Get over it? How could I? The main person in my life was gone... forever.

The Pale-Faced Girl
Cath Hensby Worboys
ISBN 978-1-78815-580-9

"There's so much darkness over this town. Can you see it?" Small patches of darkness had emerged across the town, ugly and menacing. Soon Jack finds himself on a quest to uncover the Dark forces that threaten to bring danger to his school. What are the secrets being shared in hushed whispers? What Darkness is hidden in the library? And how is Mrs Grimshaw, the deputy head teacher, involved in it all?

Books available from all good bookshops
and the publisher's website:
www.onwardsandupwards.org/shop